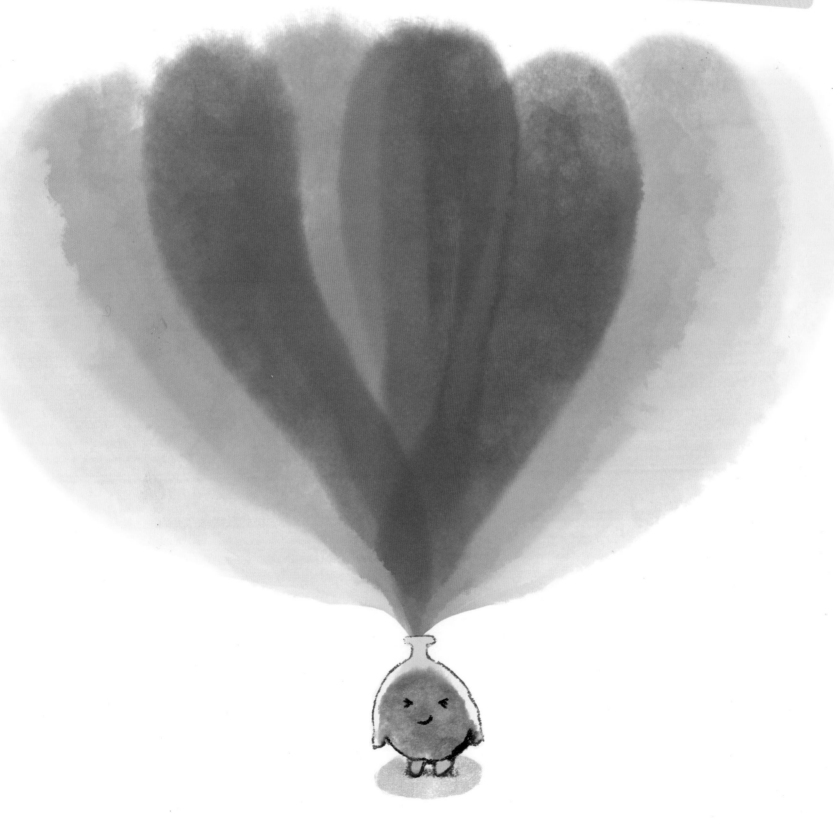

For the ladies I love and respect
Christine, Helen, Miriam, Pauliina,
Chloe, Dawn, Harri, Jo, Karin,
Jane and Cath.
– C.A.

Quarto is the authority on a wide range of topics.
Quarto educates, entertains and enriches the lives of
our readers—enthusiasts and lovers of hands-on living.

www.quartoknows.com

© 2022 Quarto Publishing plc
Text and illustrations copyright © 2022 Claire Alexander

Claire Alexander has asserted her right to be identified
as the author and illustrator of this work.

First published in 2022 by Happy Yak,
an imprint of The Quarto Group.
The Old Brewery, 6 Blundell Street,
London N7 9BH, United Kingdom.
T (0)20 7700 6700 F (0)20 7700 8066
www.quartoknows.com

A catalogue record for this book is available from the British Library.

ISBN: 978 0 7112 6444 1

9 8 7 6 5 4 3 2 1

Manufactured in Guangdong, China CC012022

A little RESPECT

Claire Alexander

Here are the Ploofers on an adventure!

They've spotted a new place to explore.

Welcome!
We love your
colourful cloud!

Thank you!

Just look at your
sweet little booties.

And the cute way you walk!

Widdle, waddle,
widdle, waddle!

Oh, they are playing
hide and seek!

We're coming, ready or not!

Found you!

But I don't want to
play hide and seek.

Oh, dear!
What's happened
to your adorable
rainbow shoof?

Maybe you should have
a lie down, cutie pie.

You ARE looking a bit
peeky, weeky...

I DO **NOT**
NEED A LIE DOWN!

I'm sorry! I was cross.
And I thought you were
a pebble.

Well I CLEARLY look NOTHING
like a pebble, but I forgive you.
What's up, then?

Someone keeps calling me
cute, and cutie pie,
and peekie weekie
and I don't like it.

Well, show them how you feel.
Pick me up, and we'll go together.

Um, excuse me,
please can I tell you something?

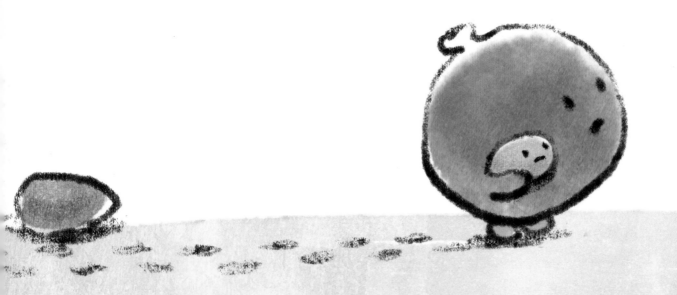

Of course, cutie pie!

Well, I don't like it
when you call me cute.
It makes me feel small.

I may be small
but I still need a
little bit of respect.

Oh dear!
I didn't know you felt like that.

I'm so sorry
I upset you.

That's okay.

Would you
like to join
us for tea?

Thank
you!

Yes, please.

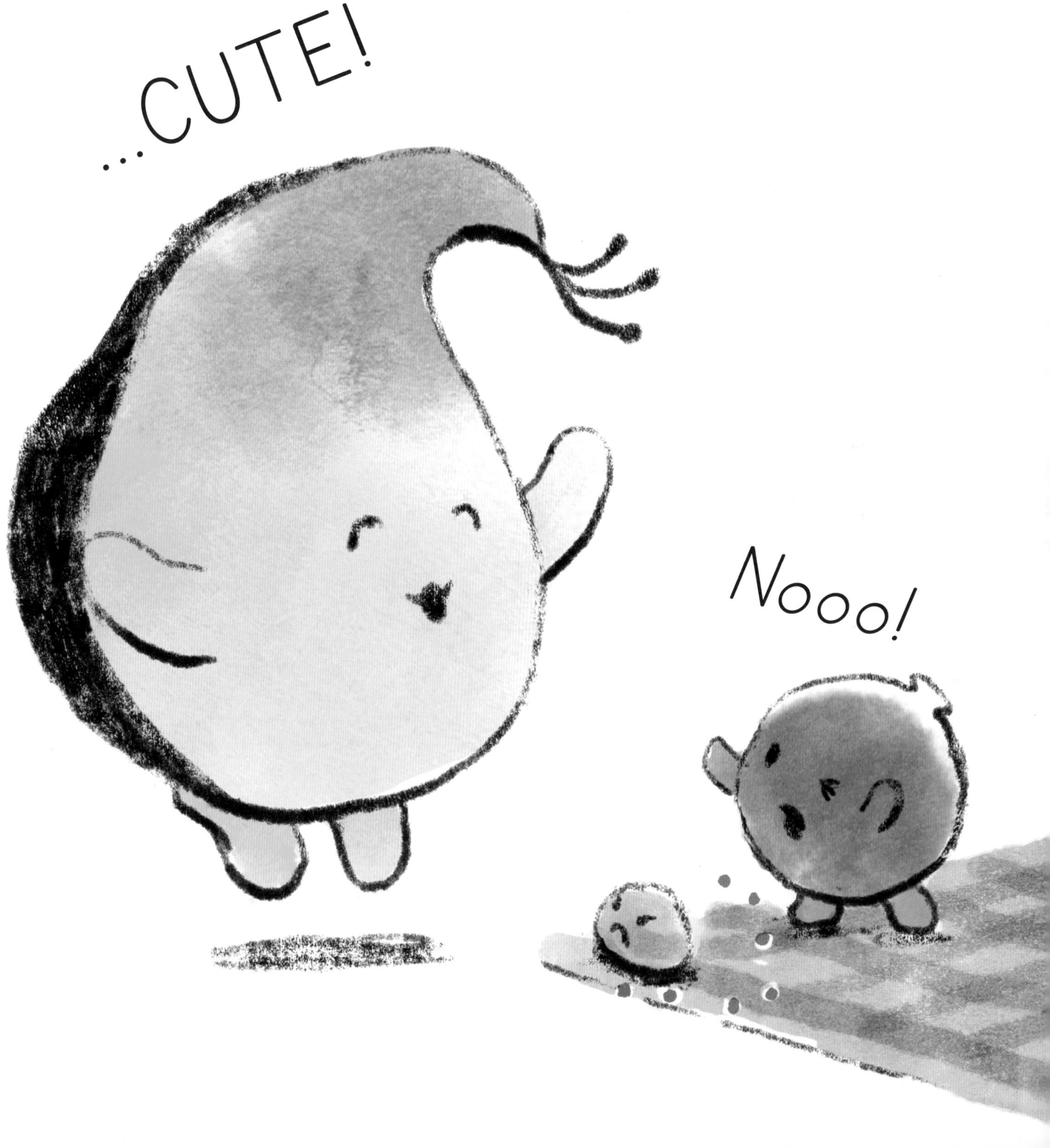
...CUTE!
Nooo!

Oops!